How Does Your Garden Grow

Also by Samantha Curtin

<u>Summer's Hollow Series</u>

Summer's Hollow
Return to Summer's Hollow
The Pascals

<u>Sergeant Russo Novellas</u>

Depraved Justice
Corrupted Defense
Miscarriage of Justice

<u>The Carmichael Series</u>
Over the River and Through the Woods

<u>The Dark Series</u>

Dark Cell
Dark Hall

<u>Standalone Novels/Novellas</u>:

Foreign Thoughts
The Scarlet Latte
Deal with the Devil

How Does Your Garden Grow

By Samantha Curtin

Published by
Behind the Curtin Publications
2410 Maytime Drive
Gambrills, MD 21054

Copyright © 2025 by Behind the Curtin Publications

All rights reserved. No part of this book may be reproduced or transmitted in any form or by any means, electronic or mechanical, including photocopying, recording, or any information storage and retrieval system, without the written permission of the publisher, expect where permitted by law.

Curtin, Samantha
How Does Your Garden Grow
ISBN: 9798313337951

The text of this book is set in 11-point Aptos
Book Design by Samantha Curtin

"All human beings, as we meet them, are commingled out of good and evil."

– Robert Louis Stevenson

Chapter 1

Eden hadn't experienced true silence in a long time. Sitting on the porch of this cottage tucked in the Mountains of Northern California was the closest she had gotten. Steam wafted from her cup of tea, the baby's cries growing louder.

Between the crying and the smell of smoke entering her nostrils, Eden took one long sip of the tea and headed back inside. The smoke smell was replaced by the coppery smell of blood mixed with the lavender from the burning incense.

As much as Eden wanted to convince herself that that smell of blood was just part of the job, there would always be that pain in her chest it brought with it. In the months following the incident in Montana – how her father coldly referred to that blood-soaked getaway that claimed her boyfriend's life – that pain is her chest became debilitating at times. Now, it was just a dull ache.

"She won't latch," the new mother said, wiping her own tears as she put the newborn to her chest.

"Give it time," Eden said in that soothing voice she had practiced so much, "I'm going to put the laundry in the washer, and I'll be back to help."

The woman nodded, "Have you heard from Celeste?"

"She's trying her best to get here, but many of the

roads are closed," Eden picked up the soiled sheets and towels, "She'll get here when she can, but you proved to yourself that you could do this all on your own. The power of a woman's body is unmatched."

She nodded, more tears falling, "Thank you for being here, Eden. If my wife couldn't be here, at least you could."

"That is what you hired me for, Aidy, to be here," Eden smiled.

"It's more than just that – you knew I didn't want to leave my home; didn't want to give birth in a sterile hospital despite all the signs pointing to that being the only option," she rambled.

"Mother nature is in fact a mother, so I'd like to think that she has spared this piece of land for you to bring more life to it," Eden nodded before heading into the laundry room.

Eden wasn't sure if she believed her own rhetoric anymore, but it was what kept her clients calm and happy. Truthfully, they shouldn't be here right now, and it was only because of the protections Eden put down that the fire was staying away. She wished she was strong enough to vanquish the fire altogether, but her powers hadn't been where they were a year and a half ago.

There was a loud bang, and Eden almost jumped out of her skin. She ran back into the living room to see the front door wide open and Celeste practically tackling her wife and daughter. Both women were sobbing, and Eden just smiled and nodded before slowly shutting the door.

As cynical as she had become lately, she did still think childbirth was a miracle, and it never ceased to amaze her the natural bond that the parents had with their new child.

After finishing the laundry and helping Aidy get comfortable in bed, Eden started to clean up the rest of the house. She had already prepared some food for them that she put in the fridge – something to hold them over until, inevitably, they were evacuated like everyone else in this part of the mountain.

"Thanks again for everything," Celeste said, "I can't imagine her being here all alone through that. Honestly, I have no idea how you were able to get here, but so grateful."

"In a crisis, I can always find a way," she nodded.

"That is what my friend said when they recommended you," Celeste chuckled, "I have to admit I was skeptical – Aidy is the one who is much more into the holistic medicine approach."

"You don't have to be a believer in the craft for me to work my magic," Eden teased.

"Well, I'm starting to believe it cause whatever magic shit you did, I'm here for it," Celeste said, finally taking off her suit jacket.

"You two going to be okay here? I don't mind

staying a bit longer."

"We'll be fine; see you in six weeks for the checkup, right?"

"Yes but obviously if anything comes up before then I'm happy to help," she nodded, moving to the living room.

Celeste went to respond but there was a knock on the door. Eden hoped it was a delivery driver or anyone other than the Cal Fire folks coming to tell them they needed to evacuate.

Celeste must have felt the same way as her brows furrowed and then swallowed loudly. She didn't even open the door until whoever was on the other side knocked again.

"Want me to..." Eden started but Celeste shook her head and went to grab the doorknob.

Eden practically held her breath as the door opened to reveal the local Deputy Chief. He pulled off his hat like she had seen him do when he had informed a family their son had been killed in a hunting accident.

"Mrs. Ogland?" he asked.

"Yes?" Celeste automatically crossed her arms to ward off whatever news was coming.

"Not sure we've officially met but I'm Deputy Chief Dealen. As I'm sure you're aware, the forest fires in the area have been spreading and are only currently at 15% containment."

He stepped back a little bit, glancing around at the trees that lined their property.

"Uh huh... kind of hard to miss when I was driving up, as well as the smoke smell that seems to have become a permanent staple this town," she said sharply.

"It is my job to inform the residents that it is in your best interest to evacuate the area."

"So, not a mandatory evacuation?"

Celeste shifted her weight a bit to her other leg, trying to remain stoic, but her fear started to sink in.

"Not right now, but in another day or two, it might," his eyes fell to Eden standing behind her, "Ms. Carmichael, nice to see you. I assume that means that your wife is either with child or just had a child?"

Celeste glanced back at Eden who stepped forward. Though Celeste hadn't wanted her to step in, it was clear that her eyes were saying something different.

"Her wife, Aidy, just had their daughter a few hours ago. She isn't in a position to travel right now," Eden took another step forward.

"I'm just trying to do my job and ensure everyone's safe, and having a newborn around all this smoke isn't good –"

"And having a mother who needs to recuperate after just birthing a child travel through that smoke isn't good either," Eden shot back.

He sighed deeply, "Twenty-four hours – if I come back and you all are still here, then I will call an ambulance myself to transport you to the hospital."

"No hospitals," Aidy's voice came from the bedroom doorway.

"Then make sure you get yourself and that baby somewhere safe," the Deputy Chief said, putting his hat back on.

"Thank you," Celeste said.

"You stay safe – Ms. Carmichael, I can see you out," he said, and she realized she was dressed as if she was leaving.

At first, she hesitated, but Celeste just nodded at her. Eden put a hand on her forearm.

"Call me if you need me," she said.

"It's getting bad, isn't it?" Eden asked after she made sure the door was closed and locked behind them.

"Cal Fire is doing their best, but with this wind and continued drought... yes, it's getting bad," he sighed, walking down the steps, "I should say I'm surprised you're out here and not having them get to the hospital."

"I just want to make sure my clients are safe and comfortable to have the best birth experience. In this case, that outweighed the risks," she said.

"Yeah, well, you're making my job harder," he sighed, looking around again at their property, "Again, not the first time."

"And here I thought you liked this whole banter we had," she smirked, teetering on flirtatious.

It was clear to her that the Deputy Chief was attracted to her and she was willing to use that to her advantage as much as possible. When she looked at him in his tan uniform, tall stature, dark hair, and green eyes, she wouldn't be opposed to a few nights in his bed.

"I don't hate it," he chuckled, "Just wish you would actually listen to us on these situations you find yourself in."

"Again, my job is to help my clients. And last time I checked, never have broken any laws," she shrugged, adjusting the strap of her medical kit on her shoulder.

"Not yet – but you've only been here 6 months, give it time," he teased, "Now I'll follow you out to the main road to make sure you get home safe. Your house and land is out of the fire zone at least."

"And here's hoping it'll stay that way," she nodded, knowing full well it would, given just how many protection spells she had in that place.

"Take care Ms. Carmichael," he tipped his hat.

"Told you last time, call me Eden," she flashed him another smile before getting into her car.

After starting the engine she quicky checked her phone to see she had no service. Hopefully, by the time she got down the mountain she would – she wanted to make a call on the way home to the pediatrician the

Oglands would be using. It was clear that the Deputy Chief thought she was taking too long but the rev of his engine.

Eden just breathed out and put her car in gear to head down the mountain. He followed her longer than just back to the main road. The squad car was behind her still as she drove down Main Street and didn't turn off until she was on the road to her small new homestead.

His overprotectiveness was endearing, but only because she had made sure neither him nor the Chief shared the rest of her family's secret. They were human, for which she was thankful for. Dealing with forest fires was one thing but she had grown very tired of dealing with werewolves.

Chapter 2

Despite being outside of the fire zone, Eden's property smelled like smoke, and ash fell on her land at times. Her garden seemed to lap it up: a mix of flowers, herbs, and a few vegetables. It reminded her of her small garden in Calgary but twice the size.

It was always her dream to have a place of her own where she could grow almost all the things she needed for her spells and even consumption. It wasn't lost on her that she picked the place in town that already had a reputation for being either haunted, inhabited by a witch, or the scene of a massacre depending on who you talked to.

After some research on the house and its previous owners, Eden found out that it was none of that and just an old family farm that was passed down and eventually turned into five plots of land, one of which was owned by an elderly woman who died in her sleep three years ago.

There was a level of otherworldly energy in this place, but it was an energy that Eden welcomed – she was otherworldly herself as it was. Part of her even wanted to see the old woman's ghost and any other forms but sadly nothing. Even one night tried to use her pendulum to talk to any spirits hanging around but no one answered that call.

So instead, here she was alone in this house on

this plane and the others. Part of her was comforted by the solitude but the other part longed for some companionship. At least the sex part she wasn't without and she had forgotten briefly jumping from monogamous relationship to monogamous relationship how much she enjoyed having sex – different sex. Most notably she enjoyed having sex with women again.

Her fantasies of Deputy Chief Dealen tying her up and taking her from behind were only replaced by the nights she had had with one of the local fire Captains. Eden had even insisted the Captain keep her uniform on while she was going down on Eden.

Deep down she knew she was trying to fill the void that Chris had left but at the very least she could have some fun with it. Already she had the reputation for being the mysterious midwife who lived in the haunted house on the south side of town. Why not throw sexually available in there with it all. Eventually she would settle down with someone again.

But this particular night, she sat naked in her garden, surrounded by her flowers, looking up at the moon, which was covered by the haze of the smoke. Even though she didn't inherit the werewolf gene, she still felt power underneath the moonlight, particularly under the full moon.

The moonlight tried its best to reach her through that haze and she leaned back onto the dark purple robe she had worn outside. Her fingertips ran across every inch of her body as if she were bathing in the moonlight, making her feel even more powerful.

Soon her fingers were gliding across her nipples which were growing hard in the dropping temperatures and made their way down to her labia and slipped into her vagina. As she pleasured herself in the garden it wasn't the Fire Captain or the Deputy Chief she was thinking about, it was Chris.

The time she rode him in the back of his car after assisting with a birth stuck out in her mind. That night it was also the full moon and she had found herself not able to wait until she got home. Later on he had admitted it had slightly weirded him out not changing out of his soiled scrubs before the act.

Eden arched her back slightly as she continued to rub her clit until her head fell back and the climax made her let out a guttural groan that made a nearby racoon perk her head and scuttle away. Her body then relaxed back down onto the robe, and she opened her eyes.

It was much darker around her than when she had started and for a moment felt a prickle down the base of her neck. She shivered a bit and pulled back on her robe. She hoped that one of the neighbors hadn't wandered over to catch the show since she was truly feeling like she was being watched.

The winds shifted a bit, blowing the clouds from

the moon and blowing in the strong smell of smoke. That was enough to make her stand right up in her garden and glance around. For a moment she thought she was going to see flames leaping across her grass but there was nothing.

The smell continued to grow though and she made her way towards her house. That's when she saw it. A large grey wolf was to the left of her house on the edge of the woods. The prickle on her neck grew and ran down her spine. There was a moment where her and the wolf locked eyes and then it turned and leapt into the forest.

"Shit," she muttered as she rushed into her house.

Without hesitation she walked into her study and pulled the gun out of the drawer. After making sure it was loaded with the correct silver ammo she cocked it and hurried back outside. She had learned a long time ago that using magic with werewolves was like bringing a knife to a gun fight – so she always brought her gun.

That instinct in her kicked in as she held the gun tightly to her side and walked into the woods. She listened intently for any rustling of leaves or breaking twigs. There was nothing, not even that racoon.

In that moment she was brought back to last year, walking through the Montana woods. At least this time it wasn't cold and snowy but the smoke from the fires had permeated these woods too. In fact, there was more smoke than just from the fires on the other side of the mountains.

As she crept further into the forest, the smoke grew until she made it to the other side where the other plot of land was being built. Or rather – had been built up since the small structure of the barn was now up in flames.

Quickly Eden assessed the situation to see that the house that was about 500 feet away was still intact – for now. The ground around the half-built barn looked stable and untouched. She wasn't an arson specialist but unless an ember from the far away fires lit this barn up, it was looking like someone set this fire.

Eden's phone was back at the house, not to mention she didn't want to have Cal Fire show up with her in only a robe holding a gun. As fast she could in bare feet, she ran through the woods and to her property.

Right now she realized how stupid she was to chase that wolf through the woods with her house unlocked and no phone on her. Instead, she focused, called 911, and reported the structure fire, giving them as much detail as she could.

After she hung up, telling them she'd meet them on the property, she put on jeans, a t-shirt, and her bomber jacket. She had almost forgotten about her sex magic ritual and also used the bathroom and washed her hands to at least wash her own scent off.

Taking her steps two at a time, she pulled on her shoes and headed back outside to hear the fire trucks on the road that led to their properties. It was easier for her to walk through the woods than to walk down her drive and around the road. She didn't want to make this a habit but wanted to help.

The firemen and women started immediately by drenching the house in water from the hose, which was already working. Captain Locke was getting out of the truck when Eden walked onto the property.

"Does anyone live here yet?" Locke asked her.

Eden shook her head, "I don't think so; a couple bought it and was trying to build it into a type of Dude Ranch. That's why they were building the barn."

"Have you seen any other signs of fire around here?" she asked.

"No this was the first; honestly didn't notice at first until..." she thought about the wolf that had led her here – whether intentional or not.

"Until what?" Locke asked.

Eden swallowed hard, "I smelled the smoke. Figure it was more than just the usual so I carefully checked it out. That's when I saw the barn on fire."

"Did you notice the smell earlier?" Locke was now writing things down in the pad she pulled from her jacket.

"No just maybe 30 minutes before I came over here."

"Were you outside?" Locke asked, glancing at her watch.

"Yes I was in my garden. I know that may sound weird but kind of a ritual to tend to my garden on the full moon," she said slowly.

"Not weird coming from you," Locke said writing something down without skipping a beat, "And you didn't see anyone or hear anything before or when you got to the property?"

Again she thought of the wolf.

"No, didn't see or hear anything," she shook her head.

"Well it's a lucky thing that you were alerted to this. Could've jumped to the house or even hit that tree line and headed to your property."

"Just lucky timing I guess," she rubbed her neck, that prickling feeling back.

As Locke continued to take notes, Eden swallowed hard and slowly turned her head to the tree line. Two yellow eyes were peering at her from the woods, and she tried to remain calm and collected. She was ready to pull out magic to protect her and these firefighters, but then her eyes moved back into the words until they were gone.

Maybe whoever that was really was trying to help her; or fuck with her, which was more likely. Again she had landed herself in a town with werewolves – whether they were already here or followed her. Her Dad had always told her there was nowhere she could run that this life wouldn't catch up with her and he was right.

"Hey Captain we got something!" the youngest of the firefighters said and he looked pale and scared.

"Stay here," Locke warned Eden as she made her way towards the structure that was still smoking but the majority of the fire out.

Eden didn't listen to her and slowly followed behind them to the other side of the barn. The barn doors had fallen down in the fire, and Eden's nose caught what they revealed before her eyes. The pungent smell of burning flesh and a charred corpse the was now lying on those smoldering doors.

"Call the Chief," Locke said quickly.

"Yes Captain," the young firefighter said but took two steps and vomited onto the ground.

"Oh Jesus Christ," she yelled, "Someone come deal with this kid and call the Chief. This is officially a crime scene."

Eden couldn't help but walk over to the body, looking for any identifying markers. Everything was charred beyond recognition but Eden closed her eyes briefly and tried to sense who this person was.

"What are you doing?" Locke sighed as Eden opened her eyes, "I thought I told you to stay behind."

"It looks like this body might have been the origin

of the fire. It's the most charred of anything here," Eden said, glancing into the barn.

"You moonlighting as an investigator while also a midwife?" Locke asked, a mix of annoyed and intrigued.

"Just have seen my fair share of bodies..." Eden said absentmindedly.

"Well don't touch anything; we need to wait for the Chief."

"Not touching anything," Eden put her hands up but looked from the body to the half-built structure, "Just wanted to say that all signs point to this not only being intentional but maybe even to cover up a murder."

"Again, not an investigator... but appears that way. You realize that your proximity to the property makes you a suspect."

"Would be pretty stupid of me to call in my own arson and murder cover up..."

"I know that but I'm just preparing you; so you need to stick around," Locke said, "And I know that you're a midwife and have seen dead bodies before but your calmness right now is slightly scary. Maybe dial up being a freaked-out neighbor or something."

"You telling me to play the part of hysterical woman, Captain?" she chuckled, again bordering on flirtation.

"We both know you are the opposite but it might help..."

"You're probably right, considering that I had a run in with the Deputy Chief earlier today."

The sound of the water rushing stopped and one of the firefighters yelled all clear. Locke started to walk around to the other side; the young firefighter leaning against the engine with a bottle of water in hand.

"Well you mean yesterday at this point," Locke glanced at her watch.

"How about I go back to my house and put on a pot of coffee," Eden said, touching Locke's shoulder, "Then after the Chief gets here and inspects the scene you all can come inside my house and I can at least be comfortable while I'm interrogated."

Locke put her opposite hand on Eden's, "Just promise you're not going to run off or skip town, okay?"

"Not my style," she assured her though a small part of Eden wanted to do just that, "You have my number if you need me."

"That I do," Locke smiled, "And Eden? Though I'm sorry that this happened so close to your land I'm weirdly glad it was you here and not another resident who wouldn't be as..."

"Okay with a charred corpse less than a quarter mile from my house? I get it," she started to walk off.

This time, she walked around the woods to the road and down her driveaway instead of cutting through. She still didn't know who this werewolf was that was luring her to crime scenes and she didn't want to find out unarmed.

She'd had enough sense to lock her door when going back over to the neighbors and the familiar sensation on her neck as she unlocked the door was a reminder of that. In an effort to either ignore it, she just went into the house and shut and locked the door behind her.

Her heart rate was elevated and breathing more labored than usual. A mix of walking fast back to her house and this impending investigation most likely to blame.

While she fixed a pot of coffee and put on hot water for tea, she thought through anyone she had come in contact with here in Rising Pines who had given her bad vibes or any non-human vibes. No one came to mind. At least the feeling of the presence of the wolf validated that her ability to sense werewolves wasn't waning.

Right now though she was suddenly less worried about the werewolf that was here and more worried about the other werewolves that might be coming. They always travelled in packs and Eden was currently missing hers to fight back with.

Chapter 3

"When was the last time you saw your neighbors?" the Chief asked as he took a long sip from the coffee with more sugar than he needed.

"Like I told the Captain they weren't so much neighbors as the ones who purchased the land," she leaned back into the back of her wooden chair.

"Regardless, when did you see them last?"

"Last month I think. That's when they started work on the barn," Eden mused.

"Did you talk to them extensively? Get to know them?"

Eden thought for a second and Locke shot her a look before blowing on her hot coffee.

"Not that I can remember. Most of what I know about them Connie told me."

"Connie as in the neighbor on the other side of the Welsh's property?"

"Yes she's much more..." Eden chose her words carefully, "In the know about what's happening."

"Oh I am aware who Connie Trent is," he smiled for the first time since entering her house.

It was the first time since he walked in that the tension was cut. Even that feeling of being watched was gone.

"What did Connie tell you?" Locke asked, trying to

hurry this conversation along as the sun was starting to rise.

"Just that Mr. and Mrs. Welsh are from Sacramento and like to buy properties up here to flip or turn into businesses. From what Connie said and the looks of the property they were trying to turn their land into some sort of Dude Ranch. I'm lucky that I have the woods dividing our land so I don't get much of the construction noise. However, Connie has more open access, which is why she knows more."

He nodded slowly, "Makes sense; honestly surprised she didn't show up at the scene last night."

"I'm glad she wasn't," Locke sighed, "Had enough to deal with without another civilian possibly seeing charred remains."

"Sound like Ms. Carmichael here handled herself well. Maybe even better than some of your firefighters given the puddles of vomit we had to quarter off," the Chief chuckled, a little too unserious in Eden's opinion of this very serious crime.

Eden stood from the kitchen table, "Either of you want more coffee?"

"I'll take a top off," the Chief smiled and Eden felt his eyes on her as she walked to the counter to grab the pot.

"Captain?" Eden offered as she slowly poured the Chief some more.

"No thanks; I'm hoping to get some sleep when I get back to the station," she gave Eden a weak smile.

Eden wasn't sleeping any time soon and filled up her own coffee cup, wishing she had spiked it with something to get through this conversation. Where the officers were slightly annoying they didn't have the same mannerism the Chief did. In fact his mannerisms and even his appearance reminded her of fake Park Ranger Roy.

"Is there anything else you need from me, Chief?" Eden sat back down on her chair.

"I think we have enough and we'll talk to Connie too," his phone buzzed once on the table and upon reading it almost spit out his coffee but instead started coughing wildly.

Despite her distaste for this man, he suddenly seemed genuinely upset, and Eden sprung up, "You okay, Chief?"

He coughed again and nodded, "Officers found something on the body. I need to get back to the scene."

"Of course," she said, "Let me put that coffee in a to go cup for you."

"Thank you," he said hitting his chest as he stood up, "Mind if I use your restroom before I head over?"

"Of course, it's to the right when you enter the hallway," she pointed past the living room.

He nodded and walked out of the kitchen, still coughing slightly.

23

"Talk about people who need to work on their poker face," Locke shook her head, still sitting at the table.

"Wonder if the body was Connie's," Eden mused, sitting back down.

"Why... would you say that?" Locke sat up taller, her interest now piqued.

"Chief mentioned he was surprised she didn't come out to the scene and I have to agree. She would've seen the smoke from her house, smelled it like I did. Not to mention he was just talking about her before getting that message which might have led to the visceral reaction."

"Again, when did you become an investigator?" she raised an eyebrow.

"Just intuitive," Eden shrugged, still trying to maintain the calm, cool exterior which was getting harder by the minute.

"Well, I'm inclined to agree with you on your thoughts," Locke said, standing up.

"I mean I hope I'm wrong," Eden sighed, downing her coffee.

"You doing okay? I know you seem so calm but regardless of who it was, someone was killed not too far from you."

"I'll be fine," Eden forced a smile.

"You have my number if you need to talk; honestly

not thrilled with you being here alone with what has gone down," Locke glanced to the bathroom door as she heard the flush of the toilet

"You're sweet but I'll be fine," Eden moved closer to Locke and kissed her on the cheek right before the Chief came out of the bathroom.

"Captain, want to accompany back over to the scene – I think your expertise may be worthwhile," he swallowed hard.

"Sure, Chief," she nodded, "I'll be right over."

The Chief adjusted his belt and headed towards the door, "Appreciate your hospitality, Ms. Carmichael. Either my Deputy or one of my officers will be by later with some follow-up questions."

Eden almost asked him if it was in fact Connie but decided to keep that to herself, "I'll be here; I don't have any clients today."

He smiled and then headed out the door. Locke put her coffee mug in the sink and washed her hands, getting ready to head after him. Eden sensed Locke's unease with all of this.

"Are you okay?" Eden leaned in the doorway of the kitchen.

"I mean not the night or morning I was expecting but I'll be fine. Just waiting for the Chief to call and get on me for not properly training Cadets or some shit like that," she rubbed her forehead.

"Doubt that anything can truly prepare someone for something like that. Unfortunately I've seen my share of dead bodies but your younger firefighters, I'm glad they haven't. Let some people in this world have some level of innocence."

Locke laughed, "You know there was part of me that thought your whole thing was an act when you first met you? The whole mystical, one with the earth, and unfazed by anything midwife. But you truly are genuine about everything aren't you?"

"I try to be at least," she shrugged, thinking of course about her family and everything she would keep to herself.

"Well you have most definitely succeeded," she walked over to her still leaning against the wood doorframe, "And if you do want some company tonight, let me know."

"If you want the company, Captain. Happy to have you over," Eden smiled.

Locke smiled back and squeezed her hand before walking towards the door, "Take care, Eden."

Eden followed her out and watched her from the porch as she walked down the drive and to the road. Breath left her mouth and she scanned the tree lines again, expecting that wolf to pop up again. There was nothing though – not even crows covering the branches like they often did in the early morning.

It wasn't chilly but Eden still hugged herself in the breeze that continued to waft that smokey smell. She wasn't sure which was more unnerving – the clear arson cover up of a dead body or the werewolf that was lingering around her property.

She went back into the house to calm her nerves, ensuring that all the windows and doors were secured, and drew herself a bath. Between the lavender bath salts and the candles she lit, she created a space that she could release the tension that had been building.

It was much needed to reset and start to work her own investigation – mostly focused around the wolf on her property. A wolf who led her to the scene and possibly saved her. Not that there weren't plenty of good werewolf packs out there, like her own family, but she was always wary when facing unknown ones.

Eden had done her due diligence when moving here – looking into any known packs in the area. The only ones that were even close, were up in the Pacific Northwest, mostly in Washington State. Very much playing into the stereotype from pop culture.

This wolf either had strayed from a pack from up there or even worse – was a rogue wolf who didn't have a pack. That made her more uneasy and caused her to call someone she was avoiding bringing into this.

"Uh oh, what's wrong?" Benton asked over Facetime as she sat in her living room, her cardigan pulled around her like a safety blanket.

"Hello to you too little brother," she rolled her eyes, "And I need your help if you're able. Not sure if I'm interrupting anything."

"This a 'keep it from Dad' help?" he glanced to his left.

"Yes please."

She leaned against the couch and waited while he got up from what she assumed was the desk in his room and shut his door.

"I'll do my best but you know how his hearing is," he ran his hand through his sandy blonde hair that her older brothers were always so envious of; they all, including Eden, got their mom's dark hair.

"I saw a wolf last night," she also lowered her voice just in case, "That led me to a burning barn and a dead body."

"Was it alone or others?" he pulled out a book.

"Only saw one but there could be others but I have no record of any packs close by."

She heard him now flipping through pages of a book off-camera.

"You're in Rising Pines, right?" he asked, not looking up from the book.

"Yes, just outside the town itself on the south-end. I'm surrounded by woods so not hard for a wolf to sneak onto my property if need be. I happened to be outside at the time when I saw it."

"And stupid question but you're sure it wasn't just an actual wolf? Not uncommon for that area."

"Actual wolves don't make the hair stand up on my body or have yellow-glowing eyes," she sighed.

"Just asking... I'm looking through my records of the known packs and you're right. There are some to the north and the to the south of you. The ones south Dad knows and I'm sure if you wanted him to, can reach out and see if any of theirs have been travelling around," he lowered his voice even more at that point.

"No... I don't want to get him involved cause he'll show up on my doorstep."

"I get it," he nodded, "There are notes of rogue packs to the east into Nevada. Problem is that whole area park land and woods and I'm sure it's hard to gather real stats on every pack out there. Not to mention, like I said, there are tons of actual wolves that make it easy to blend in."

"So in other words I could be dealing with a nomadic lone wolf, a rogue pack, or any number of things," she sighed.

"Exactly but from what it sounds like they may be on our side. Never heard of a rogue wolf alerting someone to a crime scene or leading them away from trouble. But odds are if they have any connections at all, they know who you are."

"That's what I'm most afraid of..."

"A repeat of Montana?" he offered.

Eden rubbed her left temple, "Yes; I don't need another massacre on my watch."

Benton leaned even closer to the phone, speaking in almost a whisper now, "I know you don't want to involve Dad but he may be able to reach out to one of the closer packs to get your some back up at the very least."

"Again, if he's involved I know he's going to show up at my house and I don't need that. Thanks for looking into it," she smiled.

"Of course," he smiled, "You know we miss you. And if you do need help we'll be on the first flight out there."

"I know," she sighed, "And if it comes to that I'll let you know. For now, I think I can handle it; I learned from my mistakes in Montana and have an arsenal ready if needed."

"Arsenal as in magic or..."

"Guns and knives – a whole closet full of them," she smiled.

"Good – not that I don't believe your magic works, I've seen it first-hand. But sometimes is takes hardware to handle wolves."

"I agree; like I said have learned from the past," she was starting to grow tired of this conversation and just tired in general.

"Glad to hear it; well should get to bed have to help Dad with some things super early tomorrow."

"Of course. Hope things at the Manor are going well."

"More of the same," he shrugged, "You coming home any time soon?"

"I promised Dad at least for Thanksgiving I'd make an appearance," she said.

"That's still months away," he sighed.

"I'm trying to establish myself here, set up my own practice eventually – trying to get back to having my own life again."

"I mean I get it – I'm hoping after I'm finished with Grad School Dad will loosen the strings a bit."

"You're the baby so good luck with that," she laughed, "Thanks for the help Bent."

"Of course, anytime," he smiled and then ended the video call.

Eden leaned onto her arm for a moment, trying to formulate her next steps. There were layers to this – the very dead and charred body of what she assumed was her neighbor and a wolf who may or may not be trying to help her.

Deputy Dealen never showed up that night, nor any of the officers. This could mean a lot of different things, but at least it appeared that she was off the suspect list. Still, she wanted confirmation that Connie was the one who was burned up in that barn.

For now, she decided to tempt fate; her father's voice in her ear telling her to stay inside her house. Fact was her house and the immediate grounds were safe. The protections not only kept out the forest fires but anything otherworldly. Not to mention the knife in her boot and the gun tucked in to the back of her pants, covered by her cardigan.

Out on the porch she glanced around; the smell of smoke subsiding but still faintly in the air. She glanced over at the trees and could barely see lights on the Welsh's property. Probably spotlights set up for the crime scene since it was growing darker. The good and bad about being out here was the darkness.

Eden didn't sense anything out in the grounds. The flowers were blowing in the night-time breeze but other than that nothing was stirring. After a few moments of scanning her surroundings with her flashlight, she made her way down the steps and off the porch. Then the mood changed.

It wasn't that prickling feeling of last night when she was in the garden, this was the feeling of being pulled into the earth. She felt if she took a step forward that the ground would swallow her. A dizziness followed, and she stumbled back into the porch steps, where she sat down.

Her senses were always heightened during the phases right around the full moon but this was at another level. And that's when she saw him again: the wolf standing at the edge of the words. His bright yellow eyes stared right at her and she held that stare.

Despite the dizziness she stood up and made her way towards the woods. In the process she shakily grabbed the gun from her waistband. Upon seeing this, she thought the wolf was going to retreat into the woods but instead he moved out of the tree line and started to approach her garden.

He stopped though at the edge and lowered his head right near her squash plants that were flowering. Her protection was in fact working, which meant that he wasn't just a grey wolf like her brother had suggested.

This made her smirk and the dizziness was fading. She slowly made her way through her garden but stopped as the smell hit her. Mixed in with the pungent herby smell was the smell of decay. It wasn't her compost or even the smell of an animal that may have crawled in and died. It was the smell of long rotting human flesh.

The wolf started to edge his nose into the squash plants as much as possible, and Eden's light followed his nose. The white and yellow flowers were covered with thick black goo slowly dripping onto the dirt beds. It smelled worse than the charred corpse and that feeling of being pulled down took over and she collapsed to the ground.

The wolf growled and Eden tried to get back to her

feet but that rotting goo was keeping her on the ground. She clawed at the dirt around her but she truly felt like she was sinking. Panic set in for a moment and then she remembered this was her land and she held all the power here.

Under her breath she muttered a quick releasing spell and was able to spring to her feet with ease. That goo she had felt was glueing her to the dirt was gone but that smell was still there. In fact it was even stronger now as she turned to see where the goo had come from: a half-decomposed corpse of what used to be a man was propped up against the twisting vines of her plants. She wasn't sure how she didn't see him before and shone her light up the black goo to the tattered pants of missing legs to a torso that was falling apart almost in front of her.

The jaw lay slack, the flesh almost gone at this point, and maggots were wiggling around in the mouth. Eden actually found her stomach turning, which rarely happened. Her hand was over her mouth and nose as she turned back to the wolf.

Instead of the wolf, there now stood a tall, naked black man wearing a worried look, "Figured it was time we talked."

Chapter 4

"I hope you understand my apprehension," Eden said as the gun sat on the kitchen table, pointed at the werewolf who had introduced himself as Canaan.

"I do," he nodded, shifting in the robe she had given him, "But know I'm not here to hurt you. I happen to know about your father and your brothers and fully know I'd set my own death sentence if I even touched you."

"So why the stalking around my property? Staying in wolf form and giving me cryptic messages like you're Lassy?"

Eden sipped her tea, the stench from the rotting corpse still in her nostrils even though she had changed out of her soiled clothes and thrown them right into the washing machine.

"When I thought it was over with your nosy neighbor getting burnt to a crisp I figured staying in wolf form was easier. But after seeing that... mess get dropped into your garden I had to up the stakes a bit," he breathed out.

"I will have to call that into the Chief," she sighed, "And destroy that part of the garden."

Canaan nodded, "I'll make sure I'm gone by the time that happens. Not trying to make myself known around here to anyone else."

"You mean to the humans around here," she said,

her hand lingering near the gun.

"Definitely not the humans. I have flown under the radar for the past two months and will keep it that way."

"What are you doing here? There are no known packs in the area."

"There aren't and to be honest my pack doesn't know I'm here," he rubbed the back of his head, "Was following a lead on something and it led me to your neighbor's place."

"You're back to being cryptic and considering that there is once again a dead body on my property I feel like I have the right to know what's going on. Nothing nonhuman can come onto my land without my help so are you following humans?"

"Yes – specifically the couple that bought that property. I heard you mention them turning it into a Dude Ranch but that's a cover up. They're wannabe werewolf hunters."

"Of course they are," she leaned back a bit then muttered, "Why can't I get away from this life..."

"They're responsible for killing two of my pack members and even though I promised my Dad that I would just go back to my life in LA and leave it alone, I couldn't help myself. I followed them here from Sacramento."

"I met them briefly once but I didn't get that sense from them and they had mentioned they're looking to sell anyways," her brow furrowed her skepticism coming to the surface as she eye that gun, "And how do I know that it wasn't you who killed Connie and that the half of a man in my garden isn't Mr. Welsh himself?"

"Why would I kill her and then show you to the barn? No, Connie found out what was happening – specifically the arsenal they were building in that barn. She threatened to go to the Chief, but I'm sure she thought they were like some backwoods militia and not hunting werewolves around Northern California."

Eden closed her eyes briefly, "You said wannabe werewolf hunters... what do you mean by that?"

"Think rogue packs but for humans. They came in contact with werewolves once or twice and suddenly thought they understood us. Trying to now take out any they can find good or bad and may be even trying to recruit more to their cause."

"So it's like a weird anti-werewolf cult?"

"That's a good way of putting it I guess," he shrugged, "And I'm sorry I put you in the middle of it. I'm sure that body was..."

"A message?" she offered, "Definitely not a stranger to that but last time it was a rogue werewolf pack sending me the message not humans. Somehow this is much more concerning. Anyone in this town could be part of it."

"Lucky for you since they don't know about our network, actual lore, or really anything other than what they've found on Wikipedia or the Dark Web... I don't think they know who you are."

"Clearly cause they should know a dead body isn't going to scare me off..." she sighed, trying to figure out how to move forward with this, "So what is your endgame? You followed them here, are watching them, and now that they're killing off humans you're going to..."

"That was the point of luring you over. I need your help to get these guys in jail. I'm afraid if I kill them I'll get myself in trouble with humans and werewolves. But if they get knocked down a peg or two, they'll realize they're in over their heads."

She just nodded slowly, "Do you know who that body is? It looked male but it also looks like he's been dead for weeks..."

Her voice trailed off as suddenly she stood up from the kitchen table and headed outside. Canaan was confused but right at her heels, or rather her bare feet as she took her steps two at a time.

"Eden," he hissed, pulling the barely fitting robe around him as he went.

She ignored him and went right back over to the body, which even in the hour they were inside, had all kinds of bugs crawling over both the parts that were intact and the ones that were liquified. Without hesitation she went right for the head and pulled back what was left of the upper lip. The lip fell off in her hands as she did but achieved what she needed.

The larger canines were starting to come down from the top and it was clear the nose had also started to elongate.

"Shit... this is a werewolf," he said, "But what about your spell?"

"I mean he's so decayed he's not anything now," she stood up and wiped her hands on her pants, "Probably why we wouldn't sense him either. By the looks of it, he started to transform when he was killed."

"We should probably deal with this body ourselves then..." his voice trailed off as headlights were now at the start of her driveway.

"Of course now they come," she sighed, watching the lights grow closer, "You should get out of here."

He didn't respond and she heard a rustling behind her. She turned to see her robe on the ground and his wolf bounding off to the woods.

"Well lovely meeting you too, Canaan," she muttered, now realizing that the headlights belonged to the Locke's truck.

Still not who she wanted to see right now as she stood next to a dead body that was starting to attract even more bugs. Locke pulled next to her car and Eden slowly approached her.

"What's wrong?" she asked, clearly seeing the look on Eden's face and thankfully ignoring the robe she was holding.

Eden would just have to play this off and hope that the medical examiner wasn't up on werewolf anatomy.

"Came out to get some mint for my tea and came across something more than a little unpleasant."

"Show me," Locke said pulling out her flashlight as Eden led the way.

It wasn't far until Locke covered her nose with her hand and stopped in her tracks. She may have an iron stomach like Eden but this was a whole new level of carnage.

"Oh god..." she said, her eyes growing wide, "What the hell happened."

"My take? Whoever killed Connie is pissed off I alerted the authorities to the barn and left me a fun present. Or they're trying to pin the murders on me... or both."

Locke inched closer but quickly turned away, "This is above my pay grade; let's go inside and call the Chief."

"Where I was headed when you pulled up," Eden said sadly.

"You okay?" Locke put a hand on her back as they walked.

"Been better," she cleared her throat, "Especially since I got some of the... decomposing flesh on me."

"Oh god," Locke repeated, looking down at Eden's

pants, "Let's get you cleaned up."

"You don't think the Chief will need to see this for evidence or something? To see I'm not trying to cover this up?"

"Good point... let's just get you changed then and keep the pants for evidence," Locke was now the one to go into the house first.

It was weird how they had gone from their casual hook ups to her acting like a doting girlfriend. Trauma did strange things to people. Like right now Eden couldn't help but look at Locke with lust in her eyes, thinking about taking her upstairs and pulling her clothes off.

Instead, Locke called the Chief and Eden quickly showered, changed into a long, knit dress, and put the thankfully unsoiled cardigan back on. The robe she draped over the chair in the corner. It smelled faintly like musty sweat from Canaan.

She didn't have a way to contact him and didn't even know where he had been staying, but he knew where she lived and clearly knew some of her habits. She wasn't ready to put all her trust in him yet but he was currently her best chance at coming out of this not framed for murder or murdered herself.

Chapter 5

It wasn't until the next day around 4 p.m. that her garden was finally rid of the body and all the officers and coroner staff. The police tape stayed and blended in with the yellow blossoms she could see from her spot on the porch.

"You didn't have to spend your day off here," Eden said, looking up as Locke handed her third cup of coffee of the day.

"Wasn't leaving you alone dealing with all of that," she shrugged, sitting beside her, with her coffee in hand.

"Well I appreciate it," Eden half-lied.

Locke put her hand on Eden's thigh in comfort but again her libido that came after trauma was ramping back up. Some of her always wondered if that came from her werewolf side.

"Not sure what the hell is going on here but none of it is good. These aren't just murders but slasher movie level murders," Locke shuddered a bit and held her coffee tighter, "And somehow you're still so even keeled."

"At a certain point in life all the awfulness and trauma just makes you numb to it I think," she sighed, "So it's not being even keeled, it's being way too exposed to this type of thing over the years."

"Not sure if that makes me feel better or worse," Locke laughed hollowly and took a long sip of coffee,

"Makes me wish I still smoked."

"I have some joints inside if you want that," Eden offered, "And probably some mushrooms too."

"Appreciate the sentiment but I'm drug tested in my position. On top of everything I don't want to pee hot."

"Understood," Eden's eyes drifted over to the woods.

There was no sign of Canaan.

"Figured I could go get us some dinner so you don't have to worry about cooking. You haven't eaten much today."

"Can't say my appetite is high after all of that, but I could eat."

Locke leaving for a bit could be the chance she needed to get ahold of Canaan and figure out how to talk to him. After talking to the Chief she found out they couldn't get ahold of the Welshes and they were now the top suspects. But as Canaan had mentioned, there could be others in the town who were involved in the werewolf hunting cult.

Locke followed Eden inside and pulled out her phone to scroll through options. Eden was staring at her phone, wondering if it was worth calling Benton back or trying her best to navigate it alone. What she didn't want was her entire family to show up at her house and take over.

"In the mood for Thai food?"

"Sure that sounds good," Eden nodded.

Locke started to pull on her jacket, saying something about getting a few different foods to share. Eden was only half paying attention and just said "sounds good" before Locke headed out.

It wasn't that she didn't appreciate her being here but Eden wanted to keep all the werewolf shit away from her. There was no reason for her to be pulled in; if she did, Eden was afraid it would again turn out bad.

After she heard the truck drive back onto the road, Eden stuck her head back out to the porch. Canaan wasn't anywhere to be seen, but she saw that the flag was up on her mailbox at the bottom of the driveway.

She pulled on her black flats and walked down gravel, keeping a watchful eye out as she went. At least she was glad that her abilities had been heightened lately and was hyper aware. If anyone was going to try to attack her, she was ready. There was no moment that she didn't have at least her knife on her since the barn fire.

There was also still a squad car parked over at the Welsh's land and she figured it was going to stay there until they were found. It brought her zero comfort though. The envelope left in her mailbox brought her a small amount of comfort. Inside was a note from Canaan.

Staying at the Stanton Inn Room 314. Come by in the morning.

The prospect of leaving her property alone was

enough to get her back on track. The feeling of being off by herself out here had been replaced by the feeling of being watched whether it was the Chief, Canaan himself, or the Welshes that were lingering around.

In her house she felt safe and secure. It was a trait she had even before she was fully into her craft – to make the space her own and avoid negative energy of any variety. Her bedroom at the Manor was the same; they could be waging war with another pack, yet she could settle into the sheets on her bed and feel okay.

The safety and security of her house was 100% her protection wards and she noticed even Locke felt more relaxed when she was inside the house. What Eden wasn't sure she could go back to was her garden. Even two days ago it was her oasis of magic and a place to be one with the earth. Now it was a dumping ground for carnage.

"You know if it weren't for the drought I would suggest just slashing and burning your garden," Locke mused when they were finishing up eating dinner in the living room – Eden was sick of sitting at that kitchen table.

"At least can do the slashing part I guess," Eden leaned into the back of couch, the tiredness finally hitting her now that all the caffeine was out of her system.

"There's a landscaper in town that I'm sure would help you take care of it."

"Maybe."

"How about I put the rest of the food away and I'll

put you to bed," Locked kissed her on the mouth quickly before getting up off the couch.

"As long as you're coming to bed with me," Eden smirked, though her eyes flickered shut a bit.

"I can definitely arrange that."

The two women went to the bedroom together and Locke was the first to sit on the bed. Eden couldn't help herself and hiked up her dress, sitting on her lap. Taking her head in both her hands she started to kiss her, her knees resting on either side of Locke's legs.

"You're not wearing any underwear," Locke said breathlessly as she moved her left hand up Eden's leg to her thigh.

"Too restricting plus now you have easy access," she hiked up the dress more so that it rest on her hips, her whole pelvis now exposed.

"With everything going on I shouldn't be into this..." Locke said between kisses as she now pawed at her bare ass.

"Yet you are," Eden smirked, now pulling off the whole dress, exposing her naked breasts.

"Where did you come from, Eden Carmichael?" Locke looked up at her hovering above her.

"How about we focus on where I'm coming tonight," she laughed, pushing Locke down on the bed and slowly started to underdo her belt.

"What a line," Locke shook her head and

shimmied out of her pants and thong.

Eden's fingers slipped into Locke with one move and her back arched. Eden could help but smile at her ability to have that effect on women. The past few times it had been Locke taking care of her and now it was time to repay the favor. In fact she repaid her twice before Locke pulled Eden up onto her.

"I'm supposed to be the one looking after you," she swallow hard, trying to catch her breath.

"Trust me that response was like taking care of me. It's like my own brand of sex magic," Eden teased, kissing Locke on the mouth and then settling in next to her, "Plus if you stay the night there will be plenty more time to 'look after me' as you so aptly put."

Eden started to sink into the sheets, and she realized how tired she was. She felt Locke turn over to face her, putting a hand on her bare arm.

"How are you really doing with all of this?"

"Ready for it to be over," Eden didn't open her eyes.

"I mostly was just worried that this is going to scare you off," Locke started to stroke her hair, "I know we haven't spent that much time together but I'd love to change that. Something about you I just find intoxicating and I want to learn more about you."

Her eyes opened for a moment, "I was worried I'd scare you off. I'm not sure if I'm cursed, but these things tend to follow me. I don't want you to think I had anything to do with this."

"I don't scare easily and can tell you didn't have anything to do with this. You just got thrown into an awful situation and I'm more concerned for you."

Eden sunk further down into the sheets, "Let's just hope the Chief can actually do his job and find these assholes."

"Was thinking more psychos than assholes but I echo that sentiment. Well until then you're welcome to come to my apartment if you want. Not as big as this place of course but as far as I know, there are no corpses."

"I'm not going to be run off my own land," was the last thing she said before drifting off.

That night Eden slept the hardest she had in a very long time. When she woke up in the morning she felt weirdly refreshed. Locke had already gotten up but the flush of the master bedroom toilet made Eden sigh in relief that she hadn't left.

Eden sat up in bed, her exposed breasts resting on the edge of the sheet, "I'm sure you have to get to work soon."

"No, I have the night shift again tonight," she said, "Making up for that long vacation I took last month."

"I can make us breakfast then if you have some time."

Going to see Canaan was the only thing on her mind now but she was trying to keep things as normal as possible. Her desire to keep Locke out of this was growing more, and she couldn't help but think of Chris.

"Just some coffee would be good; I don't eat much in the mornings. And was gonna hit the gym too..."

Her eyes were on Eden as she got out of the bed and grabbed a silk robe out of her closet. The same robe she had worn when she first met Canaan in wolf form. He never addressed it but Eden was sure that he had seen her in the garden or at the very least heard and smelled her.

Canaan wasn't her type, mostly since he was a werewolf, but she still liked the thought of him being under her spell. Just like Locke was under her spell right now, drinking up every movement of her body. Eden wasn't above using it to her advantage on either of them or Deputy Dealen if it came down to it.

"You're making it really hard to leave," Locke put her now empty coffee mug in the sink.

Eden sat on the kitchen chair and purposefully crossed her legs to reveal much of her pale skin and more, "Just means you'll have to come back."

Locke chuckled, "Try to stay out of trouble – I know the squad car is parked on the road just in case."

"I'll try. I do have a client today so will head into town," Eden lied, something she had grown accustomed to doing.

"You sure you're up for that?" she sat down to pull on her boots.

"Circle of life; I dealt with death these past two days now it's time to prepare to usher in life."

Eden shrugged as she stood up, downing the rest of her coffee.

"Well just be careful," Locke leaned in and kissed her, pushing her back against the sink.

"I still have an hour before I have to leave."
Eden undid the tie on her robe. The fabric fell along either side of her breasts, exposing the whole front of her body.

Locke didn't answer with words but instead her tongue on her nipples and her middle finger inside of her. She started to vigorously move it in and out of her and rubbed her thumb along her clit in the process. Eden gripped the sink behind her as Locke pulled her fingers out and sunk to her knees.

Her hands went up the back of her robe, cupping her ass and pulled her closer, ushering her tongue around her clit, teasing it before starting to suck on it. Eden tilted her head back as Locke finished her off with her fingers inserting back into her vagina. That combination made Eden's body go rigid and cum hard into Locke's mouth.

Now was her turn to be out of breath as Locke wiped her mouth off on the inside of Eden's leg, "We even now?"

Eden smiled, her chest rising and falling sharply,

"For now at least."

"Well not to be the one to cut and run but I should get going."

"Understood."

Eden closed her robe back up as she started to clean up the coffee mugs and pot.

"I hope we will get on the other side of it all and maybe we can explore more sides of each other."

She adjusted her pants a bit at the waist as she started towards the door.

"I look forward to that Captain," Eden called after her.

"How many times do I have to tell you to call me Chelsea," Locke called back without turning around

"Captain is just so much hotter," Eden teased as Locke walked out.

Eden hugged herself as if cold and went quickly behind her to ensure the door was locked. She glanced out of the side windows in the process, scanning her grounds quickly. She hated to admit it but she was feeling very uneasy about what was to come.

Chapter 6

"Twice in one week, this is a new record," Benton teased as she adjusted her phone to lean against her desk.

"You're the only one I trust right now not to run to Dad with this," she said her voice lowered.

"He's not home – he and Ian went to meet with another pack in Toronto," he ruffled his hair a bit, "So you can speak freely. Did you see that wolf again?"

"A little more than saw him," she sighed, "We talked after I found another body, this time a half-decomposed wolf in my garden."

Benton sat up straight, "Maybe you should talk to Dad."

"No... but I need you to see if you can find information on a wolf named Caanan. He's the one who was leading me to these bodies. Claims he's been keeping watch on some kind of cult in the area," she decided to leave out the werewolf hunter part at this point, "Thinks my neighbors are part of it and they're trying to cover their tracks by killing my other neighbor and another local werewolf."

"Not Canaan Bridges?" Benton said slowly.

"He a werewolf? I'm sure there are not many werewolves out there named Canaan, or anyone named Canaan for that matter," her heart was suddenly in her throat as she noticed Benton's change in demeanor.

"Yes, he's a werewolf, and his parents are friends of the family. You've met them I think a couple years back. They used to live near us but moved out west and we lost touch."

"Lost touch as in they went rogue?" she shifted a bit, running her hand through her hair, wondering now if him luring her to the Inn was a trap.

"No, nothing like that..." Benton said and she heard him swallow.

"Bent, what's going on? Why are you acting weird? Should I be scared of him?"

"No, no..." he shook his head, "More the opposite. His parents were very helpful actually in finding rogue packs, nomads, and others on the fray. Were great trackers. Probably why he's been able to track your neighbors without you noticing until he wanted you to."

"Okay so he's an ally and I can trust him?" she said looking Benton who was now staring into his lap, "He wanted me to meet him at the Inn he's staying at. I want to make sure I'm not walking into a trap."

"You can trust him, yes," he nodded.

"So, back to my other question, why are you acting weird?"

"I know him a little too well... or at least I did," Benton finally said, looking back up at her.

"Oh..." she said, nodding and suddenly feeling

bad, "I'm sorry I never realized you were into men."

"Well neither did Canaan apparently. His Dad found out... rather found me in bed with him and he freaked out and moved them across the country," he rubbed his face, "Haven't talked to Canaan since."

"I'm so sorry Bent that's awful," her voice softened, "Does... Dad know?"

"Considering Edwin Bridges yelled at him and blamed me for turning his son gay, yes he knows."

"How did I not know? Why didn't you tell me?" she asked, trying not to be accusatory but failing.

Benton scoffed, "Eden you left and barely talked to any of us. When was I supposed to tell you?"

"Last year I was there though. You could've told me then. You know that I of all people understand."

He shook his head, "It's different for you; you're a woman and already had the whole sapphic witch energy before you even came out. But I'm supposed to help continue the lineage and be like Dad and our brothers."

"You can be gay and be masculine and a werewolf. They're not mutually exclusive," she sighed, "But I'm sorry that you've been struggling with it all. You can always talk to me, I promise. I should have been there for you."

Benton just nodded.

"Are you okay with me working with Canaan? If he had any hand in making you feel like it was your fault..."

"No, he's a good guy who has bigoted parents," again he swallowed hard, "But I have to admit hearing that name five years later does sting."

"I mean, should I mention you at all, or should I just keep on going along with him helping me and not knowing who he is?"

"If it comes up, sure. But don't offer that you talked to me about it, okay?"

Eden nodded.
"After this is over do you want to come out and visit me? We can really talk and maybe you can clear the air with Canaan?"

"We'll see," he said, "But Eden I'm worried about you taking this on."

"Like you said, sounds like Canaan is more than capable. And as always, I go into things cautiously with as much information as I can find," she said, sitting back from the phone a bit.

"And you're sure that I shouldn't tell Dad? Or maybe even just Ian and Rowan?"

"I tell both or even one of them and it'll come out to Dad. No you're the only person I need to tell. I will meet up with Canaan today and see what he knows, and we'll take it from there. Meanwhile there are cops crawling around this part of town so this cult should lay low."

Eden glanced outside to see there was now a cruiser at the end of her driveway too.

"Just be careful and keep me posted, okay?" he breathed out.

"I will," she said now smiling at him, "Love you Bent."

"Love you too Eden," he rolled his eyes and ended the call.

Eden flipped over her phone so it rested on her desk. She had a moment to think about leaving and going home. When she had left home it hadn't occurred to her that her younger brother might still need her; at that time he was 18 and going into college.

Benton was making something of himself by continuing the family legacy and becoming a research librarian. His skills were well used in the family and at the University that he worked at. She was so proud of him but hated that he had been subjected to hate.

Eden wasn't sure if she was going to be able to keep Benton out of the conversation she was about to have with Canaan but she was going to try. Even though Bent had said he was one of the good ones and her senses told her the same, she still armed herself with weapons and magic, just in case.

She carried her medical bag out to the car, looking around carefully as she got into the car. The uneasiness around this place was growing and she made a note when this was all over to do a cleansing. What she had told the Captain was true – she was not going to be driven from this place.

What apparently was going to happen though was the continued watch around her property. As she pulled down the driveway Deputy Dealen got out of the cruiser. He wasn't wearing his uniform – instead jeans and a polo shirt. It also looked like he hadn't shaved since the last time she saw him.

Eden rolled down her window as she drove, slowly down as he walked up.

"Good morning, Deputy," she said up at him.

"Skipping town?" he teased.

"No, meeting a client. Should be back in a few hours," she offered.

"Would you like me to accompany you? Not crazy about you going off by yourself right now given what happened last night," he wrinkled his nose a bit as he glanced over at her garden.

"Appreciate the concern Deputy but I don't want to alarm my client at all. Everything needs to stay calm," she squinted up at him.

"Understood," he nodded, "I'll head back into town then and have the others stay here and watch."

"Still no word yet from the Welshes?"

"Really shouldn't share information with you about an ongoing investigation," he rested his hands on his belt and leaned in a little closer, "But no, they seem to be in the wind and are now the top suspects."

"Lovely," she breathed out.

"You sure you don't want me to at least follow you to your client? I don't mind. I promise I'll be nicer than I was when you were with your last client," he leaned in even closer.

"Appreciate it but really I'll be fine. I promise I'm tougher than I look," she forced a smile.

"Oh I have no doubt; to not be hysterical after finding not one but two bodies in the span of 48 hours you have to be tough," he patted the window frame, "Well I'll come back tonight to check on you."

"Appreciate it," she repeated as he withdrew his hand and she drove off down the road.

Eden hoped that the weirdness from him was because he had a thing for her and not because he was somehow involved in the cult. Since she hadn't trusted her instincts as much after Montana, she performed a spell on Dealen and the rest of the police department to ensure they weren't werewolves. But wannabe werewolf hunters was a whole other issue that there wasn't any test for.

Maybe Canaan had some more insights but she really didn't want to put all her stock in him, especially now given what she knew about his history with Benton. After all this was over she had half a mind to follow Canaan back to his home and confront his parents about it. It wouldn't solve anything, but it might help the ache in her stomach go away.

The Inn that Canaan was staying in was old but beautiful. It was tucked into the woods on the other side of town and overlooked the river. Downside for her was she had to go in the front door and wander up to his room, which she tried to do as inconspicuously as possible.

There were a few people milling around the lobby but thankfully she was able to make it to the elevator without anyone joining her or stopping her. In retrospect it wasn't great security-wise but it was a small town and overly trusting. I struck her that might be why the Welshes had picked Rising Pines.

When the elevator door opened the third floor, Eden glanced up and down the hallway before stepping off and heading to room 314. Her instincts and Benton's backing made her comfortable enough to trust Canaan, but she didn't trust anyone who may have been watching her.

She went to knock on the door when it opened, revealing Canaan on the other side clearly waiting for her. He practically pulled her inside and then shut and latched the door.

"Good Morning to you too," Eden said.

"Sorry but I'm extra paranoid after what happened in your garden," he said, shoving his hands into the pockets of his jeans.

Eden realized that this was the first time she had

seen him clothed – a detail she had left out when talking to Benton. His dark-washed jeans, white shirt, and dark green sweater vest wasn't exactly what she expected.

"I don't blame you."

She looked around his hotel room where papers, news clippings, and a few maps were covering one of the beds and desk. Eden couldn't help but wander over to look at them.

"Like I mentioned, I tracked the Welshes here from Sacramento. They like to think they're good at covering up their kills but they're amateurs and have gotten sloppy."

"Yes, what they did in my garden was sloppy, and the Connie coverup was badly timed. I'm with you, we're not dealing with any experts. I'm more worried about how many people in this town they've brought into their cause."

"I share that sentiment, which is why I've been trying to look for any signs of correspondence with the Welshes or any gatherings that seem odd."

"And have you found anything?"

"So it may be overkill but I gathered a list of all the town get-togethers – large, small, even neighborhood book clubs."

"You think a book club could be a front to a cult?" she raised an eyebrow.

"I mean I wouldn't think so but I don't want to rule

anything out," he shrugged, handing her the list.

"Some of my clients might know more about these meetups."

"I was actually hoping that we can use something of more of the mystical variety to figure it out," he said slowly, "I don't want to put any more of a target on you than you already have."

"I think we're beyond that at this point but I appreciate the sentiment," she sighed, sitting on the edge of the uncovered bed, "And if anything I think I could probably eliminate some areas using a spell or two. All my things are back at my house though, which you will be safe at. I may have not been the most trusting at first but I know now that..."

"You talked to Benton?" he offered.
Eden paused for a moment, trying to think of the best way to not bring her brother into this more than necessary.

"My brother is my go-to for most research into the packs. I just wanted to make sure you were who you said you were and weren't dangerous."

"That's fair; so he told you that I was trustworthy."

"He did but also told me to tread lightly as our families don't exactly get along anymore," she got off the bed, "And how about we leave it at that."

"How is he doing?" Canaan asked now staring at the ground, his first shift from the stoic nature she had witnessed so far.

"If you're interested in how my brother is doing then you can reach out to him," she said sharply.

Canaan looked up, a flicker of regret passing over his features.

"You're right. Sorry I brought it up."

Eden nodded, gathering her thoughts, "First, we need head back to my house gather my supplies. Once we have those, I can perform a spell to narrow down who these people might be and where to find them."

"You're not worried that me getting into your car is going to draw more suspicion?" he asked, that same hesitation from when she was talking about Benton showing.

"Then stay here; do you have a phone I can call you on?" she pulled out her own phone.

Canaan nodded and reached into his pocket, retrieving a small flip phone. "It's an old model but it works," he said with a shrug, handing it to her.

Eden couldn't help but shake her head and chuckle slightly – burner phones were right out of the werewolf playbook. Still she entered her number, texted her phone, and handed his back.

"I'll call you when I've found out something."

As she turned to leave, Canaan's voice stopped her.

"Be careful, Eden. I still can't tell if they're just trying to scare you, pin all of this on you, or worse."

"Again, it's too late to be worried about that," she

sighed as she walked out of the hotel room, this time taking the stairs.

As soon as Eden stepped outside the Inn, the smell of smoke hit her nostrils. She hadn't remembered it being that strong when she arrived here, but she may have been distracted at the time. Something else she hadn't remembered was the Deputy sitting in the parking lot. He had mentioned that he could accompany her to see her client, but when she walked over to the cruiser, she saw it was empty.

Eden didn't have time to figure out why he was there – maybe he was inside one of those rooms getting laid. Right now she would focus on the spell and if it turned out the Deputy was part of this cult, then she would deal with it then.

When she got back to her house she unlocked the door and stepped inside, immediately heading to her study where she kept her magical supplies. The wave of calm that came over being back in her home was enough to at least overcome the nerves from seeing the Deputy in that parking lot.

She carefully selected the items she needed: a silver bowl, a handful of herbs, and a vial of moonlit water freshly charged from the other night. With everything gathered, she set up her workspace, the list Canaan gave her the center of it all.

Once satisfied, she lit a single candle and placed

it at the center of her table. Sitting down, she closed her eyes, taking a deep breath to center herself. The air around her hummed with energy as she began to chant softly, the words flowing out of her like water.

The flame of the candle flickered, casting shadows on the walls. Slowly, the list of people, groups, and meetings became scorched, eliminating all the erroneous possibilities - the book clubs she was happy to see were among those.

She was left with two groups that Canaan had identified: the local gun club, which she felt was a little two on the nose, and a local mom's group that mostly corresponded through Facebook posts. The bad feeling that Eden had starting with Connie's body the other night was now just turning into annoyance. If she was about to ostracize herself from yet another small town, she wouldn't be alone.

After clearing the remnants of her spell and thanking her ancestors for their help, she pulled back out her phone. Of course Locke had texted her that she would be heading to her shift soon but that she was still thinking of her. Eden couldn't help but smile that despite dealing with two bodies together, Locke wasn't budging on pursuing Eden. If this all worked out in her favor she might actually be able to have a relationship again; it would be the first since Chris.

After quickly texting Locke back, she dialed the

Deputy's number. As much as she trusted Canaan to do what was right for his family and the werewolves at large, she wasn't so sure that he wouldn't cause any collateral damage. Even though she still wasn't sure why the Deputy was at the inn, the fact that he wasn't sitting at the edge of her driveway made it seem like he had other things going on.

"Deputy Dealen," he answered after the second ring.

"Hi Deputy, it's Eden Carmichael," she said, as if he knew any other Eden's in this town.

"Everything go okay with your client?" he asked, "I happened to see your car at the Inn when I was following a lead."

"Oh yes, just a routine check-up," she felt her shoulders relax slightly, "But I may have inadvertently found out some information you all might be able to use in the investigation into the Welshes."

"I'll be over in fifteen minutes," he said, his voice suddenly tensed before he hung up.

Eden breathed out, trying to formulate how she was going to play this. He had hung up before she had a chance to say anything more. The biggest decision she had was to decide whether to lay out all the information for him or to keep him at arm's length and just use him to ensure no more bodies piled up around her property.

Chapter 7

"Surprised you know how I like my coffee," Dealen mused as he had barely stepped into her kitchen when she was handing him the steaming cup.

"Black with lots of sugar seems to be the dealers choice around here for law enforcement," she said, sitting down at the table across from him.

"So dare I ask what you've found out?" he took a long sip.

"So as I mentioned, stumbled upon some information when I was with my client today that I thought might help. It turns out that the Welshes weren't working alone and were trying to cover some things up."

"Like..."

"They didn't buy that land to make it a dude ranch; it was going to be an arsenal of sorts and there's a good chance the local gun club are the ones they were working with."

"And you found this out from you client..."

"She's part of some of those Facebook Mom groups and has been noticing some weird messages and from there I was able to figure out that it's a mix of moms in that group and their gun club husbands."

Eden even impressed herself with how good she was getting at lying. She just hoped this panned out to be right.

"So what you think they're starting some come of militia?" he laughed nervously.

"My client threw around the word cult a few times..."

Eden swallowed hard; she wasn't sold on telling him that, but that's where she drew the line.
Dealen shook his head, "So much for Rising Pines being a quiet town."

"Connie clearly was on to them and was trying to confront them about the whole thing and lost her life because of it," Eden offered, "I just hope more bodies don't start piling up."

"You know we found out that the body in your garden had been dead a few months. But based on your own knowledge I'm assuming you knew that."

Eden nodded, "The level of decomposition alone was a giveaway. Black goo on my pants."

"Well we will be keeping the squad car outside of your house for the foreseeable future," he sighed deeply, "Or we could set you up at the Inn where we can keep a better eye on you. But I think I know the answer to that."

"I'm not letting these people drive me from this new home I built," her voice rose a bit, "And as I said early, I am capable of defending myself."

Dealen took a long swig of coffee and nodded, "I'm sure your houseguest can also defend you if needed."

Eden laughed hollowly, "Small town really are all the same. The gossip just ebbs and flows. I'm sure that's how this group got started in the first place. Heard about unsavory folks moving into their areas and decided to do something about it."

"Again, that is why we will have a squad car outside your house," his brow furrowed a bit, "And for the record I didn't mean anything bad by the comment about your houseguest. I'm glad you have someone here with you."

"Well Deputy I hope you can get somewhere with the little information I could find for you," she was trying her hardest to not show with her body language that she had doubts, "Keep me in the loop are much as you can? Given the proximity of all of this to my land, I have a vested interest in it now."

"I will; thank you Ms. Carmichael," he stood up and put his mug in her sink.

Eden thought about how the Captain had pushed her up against that sink just hours before. And now the Deputy was here.

"Deputy please, again call me Eden."

A smile crossed his face, "Well Eden... for all of our sake I hope we get this all figured out. Would hate this to be the reason you or anyone else leaves."

"Really not looking to go anywhere, anytime soon," Eden smiled back.

He just nodded, thanked her again for the coffee and started towards the door. Eden watched as Dealen walk down to his car, the sun starting to set. She glanced around her home, feeling the heavy silence descending around her. The weight of the recent events and the constant vigilance was beginning to take its toll, as resilient as she was trying to be.

She went to the window and pulled back the curtain slightly, peering outside. The squad car was already parked by the curb. She sighed, closing the curtain but a pair of yellow eyes in the woods caught her attention.

Eden went to go pull on her shoes; thinking the best way to talk to him with the squad car parked at the end of her driveway. Letting him into the house would be the best bet, so she returned to the kitchen and opened the back door.

"Come in," she said in a sing song voice towards the woods where Canaan was crouched down.

Eden then watched him shift his eyes to the drive and bound up to the house across the grounds that were supposed to protect her from things like him. The fact that she was letting him in again was a testament to trusting her brother mostly. But Canaan seemed genuine and she wasn't tense around him, which of course was a good sign.

Again he was naked in her kitchen as she shut the

door behind him after quickly glancing around. She might be protected from the inhuman but it was clear the humans were the ones she had a watch out for.

"Was the Deputy any help?" Canaan asked.

"Time will tell. I gave him the information that I narrowed down – gun club and the Mom Group on Facebook. I'm not positive that they're tied together but I fed him a line that I found out through a client who is part of the online group. Keeping you out of all of this of course."

"I appreciate that," he swallowed.

"Here," she said, heading to her hall closet, grabbing the one oversized coat she had, and handing it to him.

"Thanks," he gave her a weak smile, "Though I did like that robe from the other night."

"It is one of my nicer robes," she returned the smile, "Perfect for wandering out into the woods and performing rituals in."

Canaan sat down at the chair pulled out at the kitchen table, pulling the coat around him as much as he could. Eden though continued to stand there.

"I did want to let you know…" he shifted a bit on the chair, "That first night we met I promise I wasn't spying on you and your… ritual."

"You mean you weren't watching me pleasure myself in my garden under the moonlight?" she smiled.

Canaan blushed a bit, "Benton had told me how in tune you were with nature, and now I get it."

"Sex magic is one of the strongest forms of magic, actually. In that state you are vulnerable and can really settle into the energy. You come out stronger and calmer," she offered.

"Explains why you have handled this all so well," he nodded.

Eden thought about it for a moment and realized that actually was the reason she had been so level-headed and focused. That mixed with all she learned not to do in Montana.

"Highly doubt though you came over here to talk about magic. I know how most of your werewolves feel about it."

"I like to think I'm more evolved than the elders and are accepting," he said then paused, "But no I was hoping that even with the Deputy pursuing the cult members that you would do some recon with me. I think I found where a lot of them are hanging out. A house in town that hosts a lot of parties. There's one tomorrow tonight."

"You think that I'm going to be more inconspicuous than you?" she crossed her arms, "I mean they already know who I am."

"We still don't know though if that was the Welshes that put that dead werewolf in your garden or some of the other members. More need you to help me stake it out. There's a spot on a wooden hillside we can watch under tree cover."

"You can't do it alone with your heightened sense?" she raised an eyebrow.

"I can..." he said slowly, "But it helps to have a witch by my side."

"Really leaning into this flattery aren't you?"

He opened his mouth to say something but shut it, standing up and exposing himself again.

"I'll text you where I'll be at. With any luck the Deputy goes down the same road and confirm our suspicions."

Eden paused momentarily and looked into his eyes, "When we find these people... what will be the thing that gets you closure?"

"When they aren't killing our kind anymore," he said so quickly, it sounded rehearsed.

"Guess I'll have to take you word for it for now."

"I don't kill humans," he said as he peeled off the coat and arched his back as his skin split apart along his spine.

Eden couldn't help but watch with mild amusement as he tore at his skin while his face elongated. In the light of the kitchen she saw his blood vessels break and skin stretch until he was a wolf again. He stared up at her with his yellow eyes, and she just slowly moved past him to open the door.

He took off out into the darkness. It wasn't lost on her that if this cult were smart they would be staking out her woods, watching her every move. Problem was all signs were pointing to this being a cult of opportunity and maybe even boredom.

Chapter 8

Eden wasn't aware that she was at the point in her time with Locke that they were exchanging "good morning" texts, but around 7 a.m. she received one. Weirdly enough it was followed by a similar text from Dealen but his was accompanied by "your leads paid off and we might actually make some arrests tonight."

She really hoped that those arrests were happening at the party and that they were going to witness the swarm of police onto the house. That would at least put her mind at ease to Canaan taking revenge. He may be well adjusted but he was still a wolf. There were very few wolves she had met that didn't have vengeance in them at some point.

As she went to respond to either of those texts, her phone buzzed in her hand from a phone call. Aidy's name appeared on the screen. Eden quickly pressed the answer button. In all of the mess over the past three days, she had nearly forgotten that she actually had some current clients.

"Morning, Aidy. Everything okay?"

"We were coming to see you at your house but there's police," Aidy said in a weird monotone voice that made Eden stand up.

"Everything okay?" she repeated, now walking to the front door and looking outside.

Two cop cars now parked at the end of her driveway and Celeste's car could be seen further down the road.

"We had to move to the Inn after the wildfires got too close," that same lack of all emotion in her voice, "The baby's not doing well with this transition and I thought maybe bringing her to an actual house would be better."

Eden tried to think of how to play this, looking at the crime scene tape still in her garden. Bringing a baby to place where death had so recently been wasn't the best idea and Eden's uneasiness was growing.

"I'll meet you at the end of the driveway and explain to the police that you're a client," she was already out the door, "And I promise you're safe here there's just been some weird things happening."

"I heard. I'll see you in a bit," Aidy said then hung up.

Celeste's car pulled forward and as Eden grew closer every part of her body tensed. Everything about this was wrong, but she just had to pretend that she didn't sense that Aidy was the reason for it all.

She pulled up to the driveway where two officers got out and Eden picked up the pace. This was one of those times she hated this long driveway.

"She's my client," Eden yelled, practically running up to the car, "She's coming to see me for a consult."

"Maybe Ms. Carmichael but we need to still

search her vehicle just in case. Chief's orders," the one officer said.

Eden just nodded as she walked over to the driver's side where Aidy was. Celeste was not with her and that worried her. Why she was driving Celeste's car, worried her even more.

Aidy just smiled at Eden as she rolled down the window, but there was nothing behind her eyes; there was no emotion to go with that smile. The hair on the back of Eden's neck stood up.

The officers walked around the car, looking at it but seeing nothing but the sleeping baby in the back. The officers finished their initial inspection and moved to the rear of the vehicle. One of them, a tall man with a serious demeanor, gestured to Eden to step back as he prepared to open the trunk.

Aidy remained unnervingly calm, her gaze fixed on Eden, that same empty smile on her lips. Eden's heart pounded in her chest, and she felt a sudden chill despite the warm morning sun. Something told her that whatever lay within that trunk was tied directly to everything that was going on in this town.

Eden saw the officer hesitate for a moment before releasing the latch, the trunk popping open with a soft click. As it slowly lifted, the anticipation in the air thickened. Eden held her breath, but couldn't help but step closer to the trunk.

Even with all the carnage she had seen lately, nothing could quite prepare her to see the head of Celeste sitting in what appeared to be a diaper bag. Blood was everywhere, dripping onto the two bottles tucked into the sides.

"Oh fuck..." the serious demeanor was gone as the officer pulled out his service weapon but wasn't fast enough.

Aidy threw open the door and practically leapt at the other officer. He was younger and unfortunately trigger happy since Aidy suddenly had a bullet hole in her arm as she hit the ground.

Eden wasn't concerned about Aidy now writhing on the ground in pain but the baby who was now crying in the back from the sound of her mother getting shot. As the officers called for an ambulance, Eden scooped up the crying baby and tried to soothe it.

"She was one of them!" Aidy yelled out as the taller officer handcuffed her and the other tried to stop the bleeding.

Eden just stood there, staring at them while rocking the baby. It was all making sense now, the Mom group, them staying at the Inn where Dealen had been too. He wasn't sharing more information with her than he could, at least in that aspect. Aidy was clearly the one he was looking to arrest but the bigger problem was the others who convinced a post-partum mother that her wife was a werewolf.

That's what she told Dealen, minus the werewolf part, when he came to the scene.

"We're handling it," he nodded.

"Tell that to this little baby whose one mother has been beheaded and the other has..."

"Gone batshit crazy?" he offered.

"I was going say has been conned into this and is now going to spend a lifetime in prison."

Dealen opened his mouth to say something else but the Chief was getting out of his car and walking over.

"Beginning to think that the stories about this land being cursed are true," he adjusted his sunglasses, "That or you may be, Ms. Carmichael."

"I think it's neither, and you just have a problem in this town, Chief," Eden said, still holding the baby who had fallen asleep. "And those problems keep ending up at my doorstep."

"I'll take the baby back to the station until we can contact the next of kin," the Chief said, shifting his aim.

Eden nodded, though hesitant to give up the baby. Still this baby needed to be far away from all of this and a police station might be the best place. Eden did a quick look all over her to ensure Aidy hadn't hurt her either.

Thankfully there were no marks and Eden felt a hand on her back as she backed out of the Chief's backseat after getting the car seat and the baby safely secured inside. It struck her that she didn't even know this baby's name that she had delivered. Aidy had wanted to wait to name then baby until a week later, honoring her family's traditions.

Eden turned to see Dealen standing there with his hand on her back, "How about we get you inside while we continue to clear the scene."

"You know a heads up would have been nice," Eden moved away from him, still obeying his request and starting up the driveway.

"I really didn't think this would happen. I'm sorry..." he almost hung his head as he walked with her.

"We need to stop this," she said, "I don't want anyone else showing up on my land with dead body parts. Or any body parts showing up anywhere."

Eden had been starting to lose her calm demeanor for the past few days.

"Agreed, but the "we" in this case in the police force," he mused as they walked up her front steps, "I have your leads, which have led to a venue tonight that may eradicate all of them."

"I'm sure the only reason that Aidy was involved is she wasn't of sound mind between pregnancy and postpartum depression. They preyed on her and who knows how many other people they've preyed upon. The Welshes are the center of this and until they're caught this will continue in other towns."

"Again, Eden..." he stressed her name and for once she wished he hadn't called her that, "We have it covered. You just need to stay here, or move to the Inn like I suggested."

"The Inn that most likely has the rest of Celeste Ogland propped up in bed?" she fired back.

He ran a hand across his face, "How about we sit for a bit, have some tea and then I'll get back out to help my officers."

Eden wasn't listening to him, she was already formulating in her head how she was going to fix this herself. Notably how to lure the Welshes back to Rising Pines. That though she was going to need Canaan for.

Chapter 9

"I know I said I owed you for all that has happened but this might be a little beyond that," Canaan said as they sat in the woods above the house where the party was going below.

"Nothing will change unless we make a big enough scene to get the Welshes back here. You're the one who wanted to avenge your pack members who were killed," Eden hissed.

"How do we even know that you posting about the wolf sighting will help?"

"Because I didn't post them… Cal Fire did," she said, not looking at him, "So now we need to give them the actual wolf sighting."

"You realize a lot is riding on this plan of yours," Canaan muttered, his eyes scanning below them as more guests arrived, "If this goes south we could both end up dead."

"And if we don't do this a lot more people can end up dead," Eden wasn't ready to admit it but Celeste's death had really gotten to her, "Now we need to time this right since Dealen and the rest of the force will be here soon."

Canaan nodded, pulling something out of his jacket pocket, "If I don't make it can you give this to Benton?"

"No," Eden said, walking down the hill, "You're coming out of this alive and you can confess whatever is in that letter to my brother in person."

A dark SUV pulled up to the house and Eden stopped at the edge of the tree line. Two figures got out, both wearing raincoats and pulled up hoods. That feeling of dizziness she had felt in the garden before finding the body was back. It was a good indication that these hooded figured were the Welshes. Her plan has at least partially worked.

Glancing back up at Canaan, she nodded then stopped as she saw a brush fire starting on the other side of the house. Canaan wasn't moving or changing into wolf form. He just stood there, also watching the flames moving towards the house.

Within seconds the fire grew and seemed to attack the house like a wave. Eden even looked down at her hands to ensure she wasn't inadvertently doing this with her magic. Canaan sensed this and moved closer to her.

"I think this just may be... poetic justice?" he offered, clearly as surprised as her as flames engulfed the house.

That's when the screams started and it became clear that all the people in that house were trapped. They saw some trying to open windows, others flinging objects at the sliding glass door, all to no avail.

Eden was torn between helping them and watching them all burn but then the sirens sounded. Canaan was so close to her now she could feel the warmth of his skin against hers.

"I meant what I said, I don't kill humans," he said, "But I also am not above watching them succumb to their own doing."

"I am right with you there," she said as the screaming increased as the fire engines and police cruisers pulled up.

"I think now might finally be my cue," Canaan said.

He pulled off his clothes and putting them into a neat pile on the ground. It reminded her of when Benton used to do that before changing, unlike her other brothers who would throw their clothes into a heap.

This time she watched as the fire was attempted to be controlled and the front doors at least opened just in time for a back draft to come shooting out. In that time Canaan had fully transformed and was running down the hill to the backyard. He slowly walked around the back porch, staring into the house.

Eden could sense the fear of those in there, and she sat down on the ground, trying to at least protect any innocent lives there. She should care more about everyone inside but Aidy bringing her dead wife's head onto Eden's land with her baby in tow was her breaking point. They were all culpable in her eyes.

The firefighters, now including Locke, were trying to fight the blaze the best they could but the land behind the house was continuing to fuel the fire. Eden heard one of them yelling something about a water drop, and that was her cue for moving. She hoped Canaan also heard that since she had lost sight of him.

Meanwhile they were pulling out bodies from the front door and Eden decided to play the part of a good Samaritan. Locke saw her.

"What are you doing here?" she said swallowing large gulps of air between words.

"Was heading to the police station. One of my clients was involved in an incident and her baby was take there. Then I saw the flames and figured I could use my medical training if needed."

Locke gave her a skeptical look but nodded, knowing they needed all the help they could get. "Fine, but stay out of the way as much as you can. The helicopter will be here soon for a water drop."

Eden nodded and away from the house as more bodies were being dragged out, scanning the area for signs of Canaan. She could still feel his presence but hoped he was a safe distance away. The heat from the blaze was starting to get to her now that she was down wind, and the smoke stung her eyes.

The firefighters were working frantically, dragging

more bodies and shouting commands, while paramedics tended to the injured. Eden saw two people she recognized and was almost upset that she still recognized them.

The Welshes were protesting a paramedic wanting to take a look at them and it was enough to get the Deputy's attention who just pulled up. First he saw Eden standing there and all she did was point at them. Anger flashed over his features as he went right towards them as they were trying to get to their vehicle.

That's when the helicopter sounded overhead and everyone was told to move back. Mrs. Welsh made a run for it but Eden was faster than the injured woman and practically tackled her to the ground.

She couldn't help but whisper in her ear, "This is what happens when you mess in a world you know nothing about."

Dealen came over and pulled Eden to her feet and cuffed Mrs. Welsh.

"If the whole midwife thing doesn't continue to work out I think you have a future in law enforcement," Dealen said but there was still a seriousness in his voice.

The helicopter rained water over the backyard and house, and even those on the outer edge were soaked by the drop. Eden saw Locke relax a bit and then turn to her.

"No telling how many people are hurt in there so we really could use your help."

Eden nodded and followed her into the house. It had clearly been packed with people, many of which were in various states of burned. She started by checking the pulse of two men in the living room area who looked like they were trying to get a window open.

"Both of these men are dead," Eden said dryly.

"Jesus..." Locke muttered, "Did someone lock them in here?"

"Unfortunately looks like it; my money is on the Welshes, who just tried to escape."

Eden moved on to a woman whose face was missing but she had a faint pulse

"This one is alive!" she yelled, turning back on the caring midwife.

The other ambulances and fire trucks arrived from the neighboring towns and slowly they started to pull the bodies out and get the ones still alive to the hospital. Eden figured there were at least thirty people here tonight and about half of them were dead.

"What the hell happened here tonight?" Locke asked as she stood outside with Dealen, the Chief, and Eden.

Canaan was thankfully long gone.

"We can surmise this was some sort of cult meeting led by the Welshes. They had convinced these people that some folks in this town were not human and they were killing them off for some righteous cause," the

Deputy said while the Chief shook his head practically the whole time.

"Is that why they were terrorizing Eden?" Locke looked at her, "I mean practicing holistic medicine and maybe a little witchcraft doesn't make her not human."

"These were very naïve folks, like Mrs. Ogland who was in the throes of postpartum depression," the Chief added, "And the naivety led to tonight."

Eden sighed, knowing this went way beyond naivety. But if that's what the people of this town needed to believe she was willing to let them.

"But we have what we believe are the leaders now and they will be going down for many crimes, including what happened here tonight," Dealen said, "Which I'm sure you can back us up Captain, was not some accidental wildfire."

Locke nodded, "I can back you up on that."

"Good," the Chief said, "Now I think we all need to go home and get some sleep. We'll have plenty of time to deal with all this aftermath come morning."

"Goes without saying Eden..." Dealen turned to her, "To please stay in town until this is all figured out." Eden nodded, swallowing hard as she looked back at the charred and smoking house.

"I'll take you home," Locke offered, taking Eden's hand as the two men started walking away.

"I meant what I said before," Eden called after the

Chief and Dealen, which made them stop, "These people are not going to drive me out of the home that I've made here. And I just hope that this hasn't marred how anyone else views me."

"And I meant what I said," Dealen said sternly, now looking between the two women standing there, covered in ash still holding hands, "You didn't deserve to be a target in any of this."

Chapter 10

"You really didn't waste any time," Locke chuckled, walking outside with two cups of coffee in hand.

"Couldn't deal with looking down on that part of the garden anymore," Eden wiped sweat from her dirty brow with the back of her hand.

"I get it," Locked nodded, handing her the cup of coffee, "But you could've at least slept in."

Eden shrugged, looking back at the now flattened earth and fresh soil. Even though only half of her garden was ruined, she thought it was time to start over. Though she wouldn't leave the land, it felt off and needed to be reworked.

"No rest for the wary right? Like I'm sure you're about to head into the station to talk to the Chief." She sipped the coffee looking at Locke who had changed back into her uniform that Eden had washed last night with her ash-covered clothes. They hadn't needed them anyways lying naked in bed most of the night before Eden got up to work in the garden.

"Shortly, yes," she nodded, "Have to give my assessment of last night now that I have the report back from my team."

"Does the assessment include someone intentionally setting a forest fire downwind of a house full of members of this town?" another sip of her coffee.

"I know it wasn't you if that's what you're afraid of," Locke mused, looking at the garden still, "Haven't known you long but I can tell you truly live by the 'harm none' rule."

Eden didn't want to correct her on that notion or that she had harmed many in her lifetime. But the fact that she could keep her family's world from her was a relief. The cult may have pegged her and the werewolves but they didn't know her association.

"A fair assessment," Eden finally said, smiling, "And happy that I still haven't scared you off."

"If anything, I'm even more intrigued by you," Locked smirked, "And now I feel like this horrific case had brought us together."

"I think that's called trauma bonding, Captain," she smirked.

"Well whatever it is," she leaned in and kissed her, "I'm going to just call it a silver lining."

Locke went back inside and Eden looked at her garden while sipping the rest of her coffee. Her garden would grow back and her land would once again be protected. She could also hear birds chirping and bugs buzzing around her, a welcomed change to the silent nights of this week.

Accompanying that were footsteps in the woods and Canaan's wolf appeared at the tree line. Eden quickly glanced up at Locke, walking down the porch steps to her car. She seemed distracted, though, on her phone, and Eden shot Canaan with a warning look. He took off deeper into the woods.

"Looks like we have another brush fire on the other side of town; might be remnants from last night," Locke sighed, "You sure you can't use you magic to make it rain or something?"

"Wish it were that easy."

Eden shrugged, but in the back of her mind wondered if she could do something to help the whole town grow like she had with her garden.

"And I wouldn't be surprised if Dealen or the Chief came by today to ask more questions. As happy as I am that you were there to help last night, the fact you showed up arouses some suspicion."

"I'm aware," Eden said, "And am perfectly capable of holding my own with the Chief or Deputy Chief."

"Especially the Deputy who I think has a little crush on you, which I don't want you to take this the wrong way... but use that to your advantage as much as you can."

"Planning on it," she smirked, "But I much prefer having you in my bed."

"Hoping that can continue that you haven't grown to disenchanted with all of this."

"Like you said, this," she gestured between them, "Is our silver lining."

"See you tonight then?" Locke got into her car as Eden held onto the car door.

"I'll make you a proper dinner even," she smiled and shut the door.

Locke turned on the engine and soon was off down the drive. It was calming to see that the police cars were gone. It was just her again out here. In fact now that the Welshes were in holding and Connie dead, it really was just her.

Though Canaan appeared at the tree line again and she just waved him inside as she walked up the front steps. The door shut behind her, and she heard the familiar sound of flesh expanding and ripping.

"Thought you'd be long gone after last night," Eden mused pulling the robe off the front hooks and handing it to him.

"Didn't think checking out of the Inn abruptly would be the best thing given what all's going on. So hanging around another day and then will check out tomorrow," he said, pulling on the robe.

"A good call; thanks again for your help last night. Glad that what happened didn't end up putting us in danger after all."

"And your... good with what happened?"

"That we watched a handful of humans burn to

death or die of smoke inhalation?" she scoffed.

"Humans that wanted both of our heads... quite literally," he mused.

"I'm okay with it," she nodded, "After everything they did, they deserved it. I highly doubt after last night they will be resuming their wannabe werewolf hunting."

"Wouldn't think so but I'm gonna keep an ear to the ground just in case," he rubbed the back of his head with his hand.

"Since I landed myself right in the middle of all of it I will keep an eye out too," Eden nodded, "So what are your plans then for the day if you're not in the wind yet?"

"Was hoping you could help with that part?" he nervously pulled the robe around him.

Eden slowly nodded, grabbing her phone from the side table in the living room.

"I'm sure he'll be happy to hear from you," she pulled up her brother's number and pressed call, handing him the phone, "I'll give you some privacy. Take all the time you need."

Canaan pulled at the robe and sat on the living room couch. Thankfully the shades were pulled so no one could see in. The last thing she wanted to have to explain to the police was a half-naked black man sitting in her living room. As she walked upstairs, she heard Benton's voice, which made her smile. Perhaps that was their silver lining in all of this too.

She pulled back the shades in her bedroom to expose the bright sunlight streaming in. At this vantage point she could see smoke in the distance and she knew that the wildfire was far from over.

What she also saw far off on the other side of her property along the tree line made her heart stop briefly. Two dark grey wolves, staring intently up at her house.

Air slowly left her pursed lips and she looked back at the now familiar wolves.

"Well Dad, that didn't take long."

Made in the USA
Columbia, SC
21 May 2025